W0013898

Jo-Ann Ong studied law at the University of Sheffield from 1990 to 1993 and acquired a master's degree in banking law from Boston University in 1994. During her free time, she enjoys piano playing and looking after her pets. She lives in Melbourne and has recently completed a master's degree in international relations from Monash University.

I would like to dedicate this to my friends and family.

Jo-Ann Ong

DER WACHE MANN/
THE AWAKE MAN

AUSTIN MACAULEY PUBLISHERS™

LONDON • CAMBRIDGE • NEW YORK • SHARJAH

A CIP catalogue record for this title is available from the British Library.

ISBN 9781035864669 (Paperback)
ISBN 9781035864676 (Hardback)
ISBN 9781035864690 (ePub e-book)
ISBN 9781035864683 (Audiobook)

www.austinmacauley.com

First Published 2024
Austin Macauley Publishers Ltd®
1 Canada Square
Canary Wharf
London
E14 5AA

Chapter 1

'Mr Seel, are you alright?' asked Mr Richards as he helped him to his feet. Daniel had fainted in the candy factory, but he was able to recover, thanks to Mr Richards' assistance. Mr Richards' assistant brought a chair from the office for Daniel. Daniel sat down on the chair and then took off his jacket. Another member of the staff brought him a cup of tea. 'Thank you,' said Daniel. Daniel was a reasonably tall man with a clean-shaven face. He is forty-five years old and just had his birthday two days ago. It is a spring morning in August when he arrives in Melbourne from Munich. Daniel was still feeling exhausted from his long flight. He had travelled all the way to visit Tildam Confectionary whereby he would visit the confectionery factory to watch the manufacturing process and sample some sweets. However, he had suddenly fainted as he was about to leave.

'Daniel, I suggest you to see a doctor,' Mr Richards said seriously.

'No, I'm quite alright,' said Daniel.

'I insist,' said Mr Richards, offering to drive him to the doctor's office.

'Where did you park your car?' asked Mr Richards.

'I parked it near the parking lot on the side of the road,' said Daniel.

'That's fine. I'll drive you to the doctor,' said Mr Richards. Daniel got into Mr Richards car, slightly hesitant, but he soon relaxed as he listened to his favourite music on the radio. After a drive of forty-five minutes, they reached the doctor's office. It was a sunny day when they both entered the doctor's office. Daniel met with the doctor Mr Richards had introduced him to.

'Perhaps you've overexerted yourself, Mr Seel,' said the doctor.

'Yes, I had a long flight and only landed this morning,' said Daniel. The doctor prescribed him vitamin tablets, which Daniel bought at the pharmacy.

'Thank you very much, Mr Seel,' said the doctor. Mr Richards drove Daniel back to the factory, where he picked up his car. It was an old Volkswagen that he had rented from the airport which took him to the factory. During the drive back to the factory, Mr Richards and Daniel had a conversation in which they both would enter into a business contract. As Daniel would buy the candy from Mr Richards for possible sale in Europe, Daniel paid five hundred thousand dollars for the various sweets, which he hoped to sell at a profit in the European markets. After that, Mr Richards shook hands with Daniel.

'I must hurry. Thank you for your hospitality, Mr Richards,' said Daniel.

'That's alright. Take care of yourself,' said Mr Richards. Daniel had a similar appointment at another factory in Sydney. He was due to fly to Sydney at 3 pm. After a long drive, he arrived at the airport. He returned the car to the renter and took the bus to the domestic terminal. He got a boarding pass at the counter and sat at the departure terminal, checking his phone for new messages. One of the messages that had just come in was from his wife, Diane. *Remember to get something nice for Liesel. It's her birthday next week*, Diane wrote. *I'll certainly do that*, Daniel replied. Daniel was reading a German newspaper he had bought just a week before he arrived in Australia. It was an opportunity for him to catch up on the latest news surrounding the recent election in Germany. He knew that Diane had shown no interest in the political events in Germany, yet he sometimes asked her what she thought of the election there.

'I have no say in the election, and I'm not interested in it.' Diane would tell him. Her reaction sometimes slightly disappointed Daniel, as he fervently supported his party.

Daniel finished his coffee and went to the local stores, where he bought a bottle of perfume for Liesel, his daughter. Liesel was turning eighteen that spring and had just graduated from high school in Bern, Switzerland. Liesel now works in Bonn, where she lived with her aunt, with whom Daniel got along very well. Nevertheless, he looked forward to flying to Munich after his appointment in Sydney. Daniel momentarily sat on the couch and boarded the plane to take him to Sydney. He adjusted his seatbelt after placing his small travel bag beside his feet. A young woman with a small child sat next to him. Daniel felt the plane accelerate after twenty minutes of waiting on the runway. The plane rose into the sky. Shortly after the meal, he closed his eyes until the flight attendant brought drinks and food. Daniel fell asleep. A short time later, Daniel woke up. The child sitting next to his mother began to cry. The mother comforted the child and smiled apologetically at Daniel, but he said nothing.

Daniel often thought about how different life was in Melbourne, as he knew everyone in the industry in Munich. Melbourne seemed foreign to him. Although he had made a deal with Tildam Confectionary, he felt exhausted from travelling through Europe. Besides, he hardly knew Mr Richards, but he seemed friendly enough. Mr Richards had convinced him to see a doctor and seemed concerned about his health. Daniel closed his eyes again and dozed off. He arrived in Sydney in about an hour and a half. Daniel spent the next few hours in another candy factory and bought a few boxes of candy and chocolates. It was a short visit to the factory, and Daniel would spend the night in a hotel in Sydney, the Continental Hotel. Daniel would fly back to Munich the following day.

Daniel woke up at 4 am the following day and quickly showered in the bathroom. It was a hotel that was close to the airport. He took a cab to the airport. He was lucky that he did not have to check in his suitcase as he only had one carry-on bag. Daniel bought his boarding pass at the Lufthansa Airlines counter. He would fly via Japan, China and then to Munich. A moment later, he boarded the plane. Daniel was assigned a window seat. He stared at the window outside and saw a small van transporting various pieces of luggage to another terminal. Shortly after fifteen minutes, the flight attendant made an announcement. 'Ladies and gentlemen, this is a non-stop flight to Tokyo, Japan and the journey there will take six hours and fifteen minutes. Meanwhile, please get warm. You can order food and drinks after take-off. Please do not hesitate to contact us if you have any questions,' said the flight attendant. After the plane had taken off, the flight attendants came by with a trolley full of food and drinks. Daniel ordered pasta with beef and red wine. After the meal, he fell asleep. Two hours later, he woke up and put on his headset. He watched a Japanese program about the city of Tokyo.

Daniel looked out of the window and saw the metropolis lit up in the evening sky. It was almost night in Japan. As the plane landed, two officials from a Japanese airline suddenly walked quickly down the aisle. They announced in English that there would be an overnight stay for the passengers instead of flying to Guangzhou, as there had been a technical fault. The hotel where the passengers were to spend the night was close to the city. A queue soon formed in the corridor, and there was a slight delay in getting off the plane.

It was a warm night when Daniel boarded the bus that took the passengers to the hotel in the city. When they reached the hotel, the passengers were told to wait in the lobby at 5 am the following day and would be taken back to the airport. Daniel made his way to reception desk and got a key to his room. He was shown to a room that had a massive bathroom with a Japanese bathtub. Daniel was thrilled. He put on a kimono and filled the bathtub with soap and water. He got into the tub and relaxed there for a moment. He lay in and out of the tub for a good hour. He felt more refreshed. Daniel changed his clothes and switched on the television. He watched the news for a while but did not quite understand the language, even though he knew conversational Japanese. He looked at his wrist watch. It was half past nine at night. He stood at the window and looked at the traffic outside, which had increased in intensity. He saw the buildings that had formed a silhouette against the night sky. It looked attractive enough, and he wanted to venture out, even though he had to get up at four o'clock the following day. Daniel put on his coat, walked out of his room and locked it. He went down to the reception desk. 'Good evening,' he said to the receptionist, Yukiku. 'I would like to venture into the city and would be grateful if you had a map,' he said. Yukiku stared at him for a moment and then bowed. She handed him a map in English, and Daniel took it and smiled. As he walked out the door, Yukiku reminded him that his bus would arrive at five the following day. 'Thank you,' Daniel said to her. Daniel walked carefully out onto the sidewalk. He wanted to go to a Japanese bar. He began to read the map and recognised the direction in which he could go to. He walked down two blocks and saw a bar that served food and wine. The bar was called Asaki Bar. Karaoke music was played from the bar, where small yellow light bulbs hung from the front door. Daniel went to the bar and went inside.

'Welcome,' said the bartender in Japanese. Daniel sat at the bar and pointed to some food on the menu. The bartender smiled at him and put down sushi, green beans and a pair of chopsticks on the bar table. He also got him some warm sake and placed it beside the food.

'Arigato,' Daniel said. The bartender smiled at him again, and a waitress bowed to him twice. While Daniel ate his food, he looked toward the karaoke singer singing Akina Nakamori's popular songs. The singer looked about twenty years old and had long blondish light brown hair. She had a slim build and wore a kimono with pink flowers. The singer winked at Daniel and continued singing. A few people watched her and clapped to the rhythm. Daniel drank his sake and looked a little exhausted and somewhat alert. As the singer sang the song's last bars, she bowed to the audience's applause. She left the stage and stared at Daniel for a moment. She went to the bar table.

'Good evening,' said the singer.

'Good evening,' said Daniel. 'You sang very well.' 'Thank you,' said the singer.

'What's your name, and how old are you?' asked Daniel. The bartender stared at him for a moment and then continued working.

'Naomi,' said the singer. 'I'm twenty-four years old,' said the singer.

'I'm Daniel, from Germany,' said Daniel. Naomi paused for a moment.

'I've never been there,' said Naomi.

'What sights are there in Tokyo?' asked Daniel.

'Well, there's Shinjuku, Tokyo Disneyland, Shibuya, Harajuku and Ayoyama,' said Naomi. 'These are all very famous shopping districts, apart from Disneyland,' she added.

Daniel sipped his sake and looked very impressed. Daniel motioned for the bartender to get food ready for Naomi. They sat and ate. Naomi exchanged emails and phone numbers with Daniel, who said he had to leave the following day. Daniel made a few jokes with Naomi, who laughed politely. Daniel and Naomi ate their food and sake. He put on his coat and paid the bartender, who looked at him calmly. As Daniel left the bar, Naomi waved to him. She stayed in the Asaki Bar. Daniel had exchanged phone numbers and emails with her in case she came to Germany. It was about half past one in the morning. The cool breeze was blowing on the leaves of the trees. Daniel walked back two blocks and reached the hotel. He went to his room and took off his boots. Daniel slept for a while and then got up. It was half past two in the morning. He thought about Naomi, with whom he had a good conversation. He was hoping that he could develop their friendship into a relationship. He packed his things and went to the reception area, where a bus awaited the passengers on the flight. Daniel and the rest of the passengers boarded the bus. The bus driver drove silently and announced when they reached the airport. Daniel went to the airline counter. His plane had arrived and was due to depart in an hour. He went to the international departure point, where he boarded his plane. As his plane took off, he wondered about Naomi and whether she would visit him in Germany. Daniel was very impressed with Tokyo and would love to return there again. He rarely flew from Munich to Australia, so this was his first visit to Japan. When his plane landed in Guangzhou, he was in the airport terminal again. He was a little hesitant as he did not understand Mandarin. He heard his plane number announced in English and Mandarin during the transfer. It was good for him that he only had a small suitcase and did not have to check in any luggage. After landing in Guangzhou, his plane would fly directly to Munich in around ten hours. When he landed in Guangzhou, he felt relieved and somewhat happy as he waited again for the return flight to Munich. Many German passengers were on the plane; only a handful were Chinese; the rest were from other countries. As his plane took off from Guangzhou, Daniel looked out of the window. He fell asleep briefly.

Chapter 2

Daniel did not reach Munich until half past five in the morning. He had to clear customs at the airport terminal. He handed the inspector a bottle of perfume, which he looked at wearily and sniffed. Daniel showed his passport to the inspector, who waved at him and asked him to pass. He saw Diane in the arrivals hall, standing with a cup of coffee in her hand.

'There you are,' said Diane. They hugged for a moment. Diane looked at Daniel a little suspiciously.

'You reeked of perfume,' Diane told him.

'Oh really?' said Daniel.

Then, they walked to the parking lot in silence. Diane had driven an hour and a half to the airport and was looking forward to her husband's arrival. Daniel talked about his experience in Melbourne. He mentioned that he had made a deal with his trading partner, Mr Richards. Many of Daniel's friends thought it was an easy task for him to fly around the world just to sample sweets. However, Daniel disagreed, as he was a little tired of flying around. He also missed Liesel and looked forward to meeting her in Bonn at the weekend. For Daniel, Bonn is the most charming city in the world with cobbled streets near the central train station. He had often travelled there in his youth to spend time with Liesel's aunt and Liesel. Before he met Diane, he often travelled through Germany selling sweets he had bought in Europe. Since meeting Diane, he had travelled more internationally to faraway places. Diane came from a small family. Her mother and sister lived in London, while her father worked as an accountant in Edinburgh. Diane was about forty years old and had light brown hair and green eyes. She was very busy with her cross-stitch courses, which she considered a hobby. She attended her classes twice weekly, where she learnt to cross stitch with the many designs. On one occasion, Diane had forgotten to bring her work glasses, and she had to squint throughout the class, much to the amusement of the German ladies. As Diane was the only British girl there, she had also made friends with many of the ladies. Once a month, she had tea with them. Diane could speak a little German, which she learnt during school. So, she was able to talk to the ladies there. Diane and Daniel had no children of their own. As this was Daniel's second marriage, he was reluctant to have children with Diane, in case the marriage failed. So far, the relationship between the two has been relatively amicable, with no significant arguments. Diane liked Liesel and sometimes called her often, much to the dismay of Liesel, who was very reserved.

Daniel drove home in the car. Diane, who sat next to him, remained silent. Daniel and Diane live in a bungalow house on the city's outskirts. Daniel's cat was sitting on the windowsill while his dog wagged his tail quietly as Daniel entered the house. Diane went into the kitchen and made a pot of tea. Diane went to her room while Daniel stayed in the kitchen and drank the rest of the tea. Daniel went into the bathroom and took a shower. He felt refreshed and reviewed his contract with Mr Richards in Melbourne. Shortly after four o'clock in the afternoon, he received an email from Mr Richards.

Dear Daniel, I trust you are doing well with this email. I am sending about two boxes of the strip candy this week, which will arrive in about two days via DHL. I am grateful for your attention and look forward to talking to you this summer.

Yours sincerely,
Tom Richards.

Daniel replied and thanked Mr Richards for his promptness. The striped sweet was very popular in Melbourne, and Daniel hoped it would sell well in Munich. However, it was still too early to tell whether the sales would be successful. In the meantime, Daniel signed another contract with the supermarkets in Munich, allowing him to sell the sweets there directly. Daniel had been in the business for over twenty years, so he naturally exported some sweets to Europe. Diane was in the kitchen preparing beef stew. She put the stew on the dining table shortly after half past six in the evening. Daniel was watching the news on the television. He came to the table and sat down.

'Did you do much while I was away?' he asked.

'Not much,' said Diane. 'Did you get Liesel a present?' She asked.

'Yes, I did, actually,' said Daniel.

'Did Andrea call you?' asked Diane.

'No,' said Daniel.

'But I would go to Bonn this weekend to meet her and Liesel,' he added.

Diane remained silent. In the meantime, they had both finished their dinner. Diane put the dishes in the dishwasher while Daniel retired to his room. It was after half past nine in the evening. An owl flew past their house and gave a little hoot. Shortly afterwards, Diane put on her pyjamas and fell asleep. Daniel was already snoring.

Chapter 3

Daniel did not wake up until half past seven the following day in the morning. Diane was in the kitchen making breakfast. Daniel went to the bathroom, showered, and put on his shirt and trousers. He went into the study and switched on his computer. He received an email from Naomi.

Hello, Daniel. I thought of writing and checking in to see how you're doing. I'm singing a lot and will work with the music producers on my first album. I want to thank you for that evening. It was a pleasure to meet you.

Yours sincerely,
Naomi.

Daniel was delighted to receive her email. There was a certain attraction between the two of them. Although, he knew Diane would object to their correspondence, he wrote to Naomi anyway and thanked her for her email. Diane put the plate with the fried omelette on the table.

Meanwhile, Daniel read the newspaper. He went to the table and ate his breakfast. Daniel had an important meeting with the buyers of the sweets that morning. He was to meet with various members of the supermarket and stores. He finished his breakfast and told Diane he would return at three o'clock in the afternoon. He drove to the meeting, which was held in a building near the centre of town. He arrived at the facility at ten o'clock in the morning. He saw Mr Steinbeck and Mr Schalter having a cup of coffee. 'Hello, Daniel,' said Mr Steinbeck.

'What did you bring for us this morning?' Daniel took out some samples of the sweets and put them on the table. Mr Schalter looked impressed.

'How does this striped candy taste?' he asked Daniel. 'Here, try some.' Both men tried the candy.

'It's good,' said Mr Schalter. Meanwhile, Mr Steinbeck wanted to know how much he was selling the candy for.

'Simple,' said Daniel. 'A hundred thousand for ten boxes.'

Mr Steinbeck frowned a little. 'That's expensive,' he said. He nonetheless agreed to the sale.

Meanwhile, Mr Schalter was already busy writing a cheque for Daniel. He owned several chocolate stores in Munich and said that customers would welcome this kind of candy with the arrival of autumn. Mr Steinbeck reluctantly took out his chequebook and gave Daniel the remaining fifty thousand dollars. Afterwards, he looked a little more satisfied as he tasted a sweet. Mr Steinbeck was the owner of a supermarket chain in Munich. He had an exquisite selection of sweets for sale, and many customers bought large quantities from him during Christmas. Daniel did not want to disappoint Mr Steinbeck.

'You won't regret it. The packaging and the taste are excellent,' said Daniel.

Mr Steinbeck smiled slightly. Both Mr Steinbeck and Mr Schalter left the building shortly afterwards.

Daniel said he would deliver the boxes to them in about two days as he was waiting for the delivery from Sydney. The sale was successful, and Daniel had built a good reputation as a businessman over the years. Daniel arrived home around half past one in the afternoon. By this time, Diane had gone to her cross-stitch class. Daniel switched on his computer and wrote an email to Naomi.

Dear Naomi, I am very impressed with your singing and happy to support you in your efforts to produce your first album. I would also be delighted if you could come to Germany for a visit shortly.

Yours sincerely,
Daniel.

Daniel sent the email. Sometimes, he thought about Naomi and how he would like to revisit Japan. He liked Naomi but did not want to offend Diane, who was easily jealous. He knew it would be complicated, but he preferred to keep things simple. Diane came back from her lesson. She had tried to ask Daniel who he had met on his last trip. She feared he would run away, as she had seen many families do. Daniel did not tell her anything. He could not imagine that she knew and she would ask him lots of questions. Not only would that disturb the peace between them, but it would also make no sense for his career. Diane remained reserved in her questions. She knew that Daniel had had affairs in the past, or rather, she suspected that he had. However, he would never admit it to her. Instead, he would tell her that she was imagining too much. She was too busy with her sewing lessons to want to leave him and return to England. To put it better, she did not want to give up her life in Munich after living here for more than six years. Daniel did not try to talk to Diane about his travels. Instead, he focused on talking to her about her day and what she was doing. For a while, Diane thought she meant something special to Daniel because he would only speak to her about her life and goals. Diane did not like Andrea either. Although she suspected that she was more than just an aunt to Liesel, she did not ask Daniel too many questions about it. Diane greeted Daniel and went into her room. She put her bag on the floor and went into the kitchen. She started to bake a chicken pie for dinner. She added eggs, salt and baking powder to the flour while the chicken was cooked in the pot. She could have been a more modern woman because she believed the kitchen should be a woman's place. Daniel liked this quality about her as he was a traditional person. As usual, Daniel watched the news on the television, while Diane cooked. He loved his freedom as he did not want to feel restricted. Diane did not make him feel restricted either, as she thought that she was fine while she was with him. It was a compromise between couples that Daniel sometimes thought about. He did not feel like he was letting Diane down by writing to Naomi, for example, or visiting Andrea and Liesel at the weekend.

Chapter 4

It was a Friday evening. Daniel was packing a small suitcase for the trip to Bonn. Diane watched him pack.

'How many more days would it take for your travel?' asked Diane.

'A couple of days,' said Daniel. Diane then went into the kitchen and left Daniel to pack. After that, Daniel said bye to Diane and he drove to the central station where the night train would take him to Bonn. He would reach Bonn after midnight. Diane would be spending the weekend alone again. She began to wonder if her marriage was worth it. She knew that Daniel would stay with Andrea and Liesel. Sometimes, she was so jealous that she felt like she should stalk him. Daniel knew all this, as he had been with Diane for seven years. However, nothing could stop Daniel from visiting his daughter, who turned eighteen that weekend. Five minutes after midnight, Daniel arrived in Bonn. Andrea and Liesel were at the station to pick him up.

'You're on time,' said Andrea.

'Yes,' said Daniel. 'How are you two?' asked Daniel. 'We're fine,' said Andrea. 'We're pleased to see you,' added Andrea.

Liesel smiled cheekily at her father. They walked over the cobblestones to Andrea's car. It was a reasonably short drive to Andrea's house. Daniel was going to spend the weekend there. Liesel was going to have a little party over at the house. The following day, Daniel woke up to the smell of breakfast from the kitchen. Liesel had gone to the supermarket to get something to eat. Daniel had his breakfast. Andrea poured him a cup of coffee.

'How is business going?' asked Andrea.

'It's going well,' said Daniel. Daniel told Andrea about his trip and how he had to see a doctor there in Melbourne. 'It must have been a very long journey to Melbourne,' said Andrea.

'It was. I didn't realise it was almost spring there. It felt a bit cold there,' said Daniel.

Shortly after half past eleven, Liesel returned home. She had bought some snacks, cheese and sausages. Liesel was eighteen years old that day. She had met a classmate while working in Bonn. They had been seeing each other for about six months, and Liesel wanted to introduce him to her father. Daniel suspected that his daughter would like to introduce him to someone special. Half an hour later, Johannes arrived with a bouquet of roses for Liesel.

'Father, I'd like you to meet Johannes,' said Liesel.

Daniel shook Johannes's hand. He looked like a young lad of twenty-five years old and had dark brown hair. Johannes was happy to meet Liesel's father, whom Liesel often mentioned finally. They all ate lunch.

Daniel looked at his phone and saw a message from Diane. He did not look at the message again but talked to Johannes instead. Johannes was an engineer who worked for

Deutsche Telekom. Liesel, meanwhile, worked in a hotel bakery. She worked in the hospitality industry. They both got on very well. Johannes certainly had Daniel's approval. After lunch, they all went for a walk outside. Daniel started to have fun, as the pace of life in Bonn was much slower than in Munich. He was also a little relieved to be in Bonn when Diane began to give him the cold shoulder. He spoke to Andrea and wrote her a cheque. It was money that he would give to Liesel for her stay with Andrea in Bonn. Andrea was very grateful that Daniel could be so generous. She also knew that he did good business all over the world. Daniel stayed with Liesel and Andrea until midday on Sunday. Then he packed his bag and was ready to return to Munich when he received a message from Naomi. She said that she would be coming to Germany in a few days to visit. Daniel expected her to come here, but Naomi added that it was strictly for business, as the producers wanted her to come here to take some photos for her new album. Daniel wrote back and said that he would meet her when she arrived. Andrea and Liesel saw Daniel off at the station at one o'clock in the afternoon. It was a long journey back, and Daniel had bought a newspaper to read. Liesel had given him a cake from the bakery, which she said was just for him. It was a short visit to Bonn, but Daniel was pleased because he felt better and refreshed.

Chapter 5

Daniel did not reach Munich until six o'clock in the evening. He took a bus home and saw a rather lonely-looking Diane at the door. He saw a bunch of yellow flowers in the living room and asked who they were from.

'Mr Schalter,' said Diane.

Daniel smirked softly and went into his room. Diane looked a little angry by now. She wanted to know where he had been in Bonn. Daniel knew that Mr Schalter liked Diane. At this point, he did not care what Mr Schalter had told Diane. There was a heated argument between Daniel and Diane. Daniel pointed to the yellow flowers and almost stuttered with words while Diane said he had an affair while away. Daniel said he did not want to discuss it much, which annoyed Diane, who insisted that he had strayed. Diane retrieved some luggage from her room and said she was leaving him for good. Daniel was not stupid because he knew Mr Schalter would play a role in this scenario. Daniel and Diane got into an argument, which Daniel knew would spell the end of their relationship. Diane put on her coat and left the house with her luggage. But Daniel didn't know Mr Schalter was waiting for her in a car. He ran out of the house and saw a black car speeding away. At that moment, he knew that his marriage had failed. Daniel was devastated that Diane had just left him like that. He sat down in the chair and drank a cup of tea. He had never seen her in such a state and wondered what on earth Mr Schalter had said to her. In the long run, he was not prepared to take Diane back because he knew she had strayed herself. In the meantime, Mr Schalter had bought two tickets to London and offered to take Diane back there. Diane had immediately accepted his proposal, but Daniel had no idea. Daniel had the feeling that his world was collapsing on top of him. It was not because he did not care about Diane; they somehow had a bizarre marriage that he thought only Diane could accept. He was not pursuing Diane as he knew she had gone with Mr Schalter. He sat at his table and thought about things for a moment. He wondered where on earth he could find Diane. He knew, however, that this meant the end of his marriage to Diane. Suddenly, the doorbell rang. He entered the living room and saw his neighbour, Mr Schmidt, looking at him rather warily.

'I hope you're all right, Mr Seel,' said his neighbour in a worried voice.

'Thank you, Mr Schmidt,' said Daniel. 'Did you see Mr Schalter here this weekend?' asked Daniel.

'Yes, there was a gentleman here at the weekend,' said Mr Schmidt.

Mr Schmidt looked embarrassed because he knew that Diane often had Mr Schalter in the house. He was afraid to tell him because he did not want to upset him. He invited Mr Schmidt into his house and made him tea. He said he would make peace with Diane if she contacted him again. Mr Schmidt smiled mysteriously, knowing that Daniel had found someone outside her marriage. Still, he comforted Daniel and told him he was right next door and to listen to him if he needed someone to talk to. Mr Schmidt knew Daniel as a teenager, as he had been his neighbour for almost twenty years. Daniel had lived in his parents' house since he was a teenager. Mr Schmidt was now a grandfather. He was quite curious when Diane moved in, but now he knew she had left him. Mr Schmidt left Daniel alone as he returned to his house. Daniel started to tidy up his house and realised that the door to the shower was broken. He was disappointed in Mr Schalter and Diane because he now knew that he had been in his house during his stay in Bonn. He looked at his phone again but received no more texts from Diane. He knew Naomi would be visiting him in a few days. He liked Naomi, although he did not know her very well. He had only met her once but was very impressed by her singing and her goal of recording an album with a record company. Daniel decided to take it easy from now on. The next day, he was still cleaning his house when the post arrived. He saw a postcard from Naomi and a few bills he had to pay. He wondered where on earth Diane would be now. But he was not ready to take her back. He looked miserably at his house and had the handyman fix the shower door. He could not believe his luck and decided that from now on, he should be a little smarter about his business. He sat around his house sipping his tea. He did not feel ready to travel again to taste more sweets. Around two o'clock in the afternoon, he suddenly heard a knock on the door. Naomi came in. She stood there, a little embarrassed because his house was still chaotic.

'Hello,' said Daniel. 'I've been expecting you,' he added.

'Hello,' said Naomi. 'What happened to your house?' she asked.

'My wife left me,' he said suddenly.

'Oh,' Naomi said, a little surprised because she thought he was still single. He invited Naomi into his house and made tea for her. Naomi tried to cheer him up, but she could tell he was sad.

'Don't worry about it,' Daniel told her.

Naomi said she had taken the photos, and the producers had given her some time off to visit him. She said it was an album that would be produced in about two months.

'I didn't know you were so famous in Japan,' Daniel said. Naomi smiled sweetly at him.

'Well, I'm a working modern woman,' said Naomi.

As he and Naomi talked, she slowly became comfortable with him, knowing it was not the right time to get into anything serious. Besides, Daniel admitted that he liked her. While they were both talking, Daniel asked her to stay for dinner. Naomi helped Daniel clean up the mess in his house, as the couple had a certain attraction. Daniel was very grateful to her because he knew she meant what she had told him. Besides, it was a romance that was not easy to find. As they ate dinner, Daniel knew he had found someone special in his life because Naomi had travelled all this way to see him. He also did not want to disappoint her because he told her more about his life. Naomi listened to him with a twinkle in her eye. She was due to leave for Japan tomorrow. Daniel said that it was his turn to visit her. The only thing he feared was a backlash from Diane. But Naomi told him to take it easy. For Daniel, a man who had seemingly just woken up from a dream, he was about to embark on another long journey that he hoped would be with Naomi. As a conscious man, he knew that his priorities in life would be different this time. With this understanding, he breathed a sigh of relief as he drove Naomi to the airport. He would be visiting her soon.

Chapter 6

Daniel drove home after dropping Naomi off at the airport. He met up with some of her producers, who smiled politely at him. Naomi said that she would wait for his visit. She would stay with her parents in Tokyo, whom she would introduce him to. Although, she knew Daniel was having problems with his marriage, she did not want to interfere too much. She said goodbye to Daniel in tears and said she would wait for him. Daniel, on the other hand, had a lot to do. When Diane left the house, he wanted to look for Mr Schalter in London and ask him why he had taken her. Although, he knew they were both seeing each other behind his back, he wanted to end the marriage in court as he felt it was broken beyond repair. He bought a return ticket to London and booked his accommodation in a hotel. He knew that Mr Schalter had several businesses in London. Therefore, finding him would be fine. He packed some clothes in a suitcase, left his dog and cat in Mr Schmidt's care and drove to the airport himself. He hadn't expected Diane to misbehave. Firstly, he did not want to enter a marriage where he would be a third party. He would wish Diane to be in Mr Schalter's care. Then again, he seemed to have anticipated that his marriage would not last and had ended sooner than he had thought. He hurried to the airport and got his boarding pass at the airline counter. He boarded the plane and flew to London, a journey that would take four hours. In the meantime, he tried to contact Mr Schalter by email and only received a terse reply. The email said that Mr Schalter would meet him at his hotel. Daniel thought looking for Naomi as a potential life partner was right. Although, he knew she was a famous singer in Japan, she seemed like a person who would remain faithful to him.

Daniel had never directly cheated on Diane in all his travels. So, it surprised him that she would behave the way she did. Daniel arrived at his hotel, the London Guest House. He saw Mr Schalter pacing restlessly at the reception desk. 'Here you are, Daniel,' he said. Daniel looked him up and down and asked where Diane was.

'She's at my house,' said Mr Schalter.

'I'm sorry, but I want to be with Diane. I know she's your wife, but I understand that your marriage is irreparably broken,' Mr Schalter said.

'Mr Schalter, I don't want to argue with you here. You should have told me earlier that you were with Diane,' Daniel said, a little hurt.

Mr Schalter took out the divorce papers and put them on the table for Daniel to sign. Daniel looked at the documents and signed the divorce papers without a single word. He glared at Mr Schalter, who said that he would give the documents to Diane. It certainly meant not only the end of this relationship with Diane but also the end of their business relationship. Mr Schalter only looked at Daniel briefly and left the London Guesthouse. Daniel went to his room and unpacked his clothes. He showered and then left the hotel, walking through Covent Garden. He thought about things and how he felt he could now travel to Japan to see Naomi. Although, he knew Naomi was very busy professionally, she always made time to write to him, which he was delighted about. He felt that she was a change from Diane, but he did not want to compare her to Diane in that respect. He knew it would be another new beginning for him. He walked through the city and bought a pair of pants and a shirt. He even bought an engagement ring from a piece of jewellery he wanted to take to Japan. He was due to fly back to Munich in the evening. He felt a little tired and went back to the London Guesthouse. He took a short nap and woke up about an hour later. He switched on the television and watched the news. Suddenly, he saw the advertisement that had just come on and saw Naomi singing in the advertisement. It was an advertisement for an orange juice drink that Naomi was promoting. He observed the advertisement and was more impressed by it than ever. He did not know that Japan had produced this orange juice drink, which was becoming increasingly popular among the European young people. He was curious about the juice drink and went to the café to see if he could get one. He managed to buy one at the supermarket and tried it. It felt refreshing and full of minerals and vitamins; he thought it would serve the public as a daily drink. He went back to his hotel and packed his bag. He took the train back to the airport, where he checked in once more at the counter. He boarded the plane around half past six that same day.

Daniel reached Munich around half past nine at night and drove back to his house. It had been a very exhausting day, and he felt like a single man again for once. His house was now clean and tidy, and he went to Mr Schmidt's house and took his dog and cat with him. He thanked Mr Schmidt and gave him a box of chocolates he bought in London. Mr Schmidt looked at him worriedly and asked if everything was alright. Daniel said he was now divorced as the papers had been served on him in London. Mr Schmidt looked horrified, as he had not expected Diane to behave so rudely. Daniel said everything was settled, and he didn't want to be associated with Diane again. However, he would send the rest of her things home to Mr Schalter. Daniel had behaved like a gentleman. He was a mature man in that he did not want to upset Mr Schalter and Diane anymore after he knew they were together. In this case, he felt that there was no point in making a mountain out of a molehill. Daniel had to work the next day. With the rest of his boxes of sweets, he drove to the various candy stores in Munich and asked if they would buy them from him. The following day, he got up, dressed and drove to a store on the city outskirts that sold all sorts of goodies, such as toys and sweets. He met with the shopkeeper, who preferred to buy the rest of the sweets from him. He said it would sell well during the Oktoberfest season, and he expected a lot of tourists to stop by his store. Daniel half wished his personal life would go as smoothly as his business. Daniel was due to visit Naomi next week. He was looking forward to the visit and was glad that he could leave the country again after the end of his marriage to Diane. Naomi had been writing to him daily, telling him she was working on an album. When the next week came, Daniel travelled to Japan on a Tuesday morning.

Chapter 7

Daniel arrived in Tokyo on Wednesday evening. Naomi was there to pick him up. Both Daniel and Naomi were pleased to see each other again. However, Naomi had a bodyguard following her. The bodyguard also acted as Naomi's chauffeur. The bodyguard, named Kim, looked at Daniel calmly. Daniel tried to avert his gaze. The couple got into a white Mitsubishi car, and Kim drove it to Naomi's house, which was near the city of Tokyo. Naomi's father worked in the civil service, while her mother was a housewife. Naomi was an only child. However, she had many cousins. Kim dropped Naomi and Daniel off at the door and told her he would pick her up at nine o'clock in the morning the following day.

Kim was a tall Japanese man who had previously practised sumo wrestling. Naomi's mother was standing outside the door. She bowed to Daniel, who reciprocated. Naomi introduced Daniel to her mother and father. Daniel shook her father's hand. Daniel took off his shoes before entering the living room. Neither of Naomi's parents spoke English. Her mother, however, spoke a little German, as her great-grandmother was German. During the war, Naomi's grandmother had worked as an interpreter. As a result,

Naomi's mother could speak German relatively well. She spoke a little German with Daniel and asked him where he lived. Daniel said he lived in Munich and was very happy to meet her. Naomi was still working on her album and had to be in the office from nine o'clock in the morning until three o'clock in the afternoon. During this time, Daniel spent some time with her parents. Daniel was a little worried and wanted to make a good impression on her parents. Naomi told him not to worry because her parents were very easy-going. Daniel ate sushi prepared by her mother and a bowl of tempura noodles. It tasted delicious. Daniel enjoyed the dinner with her parents. After dinner, Naomi showed him to his room, which served as a guest room. Daniel slept most of the time. When morning came, Naomi got dressed for work and woke him up. He kissed her gently on the cheek, and Naomi said she would return at three in the afternoon. Daniel got up and showered in the bathroom. Naomi's father had already left for work, and only her mother was in the house.

'Good morning,' Daniel said in Japanese.

'Good morning,' said Naomi's mother. She made breakfast for him, which he ate. During the day, Daniel watched Naomi's mother attend to the Japanese flower arrangements which was her hobby. Daniel even helped her mother cut the leaves and trim the stems. Around two o'clock in the afternoon, Naomi's father returned home. He brought a newspaper and gave it to Daniel. It was a newspaper in German that her father had bought at a newsstand. Daniel thanked her father. Her father tried to talk to Daniel in Japanese, which Daniel understood. He told her father that he was pretty serious about his daughter. Her father looked more amused than worried. He also told the father that he was recently divorced. Naomi's mother began to look a little concerned. She asked where his wife was. He said she had left him for his business partner and was now living in London. Her father, however, did not seem worried at all. He was a happy man and took things easy. Naomi came back around three o'clock in the afternoon. She asked how his day had been. Daniel said it had been outstanding. Naomi kissed him on the cheek and went to her room to change. Afterwards, Naomi and Daniel went for a walk in the city. Naomi showed Daniel the sights of the city. They went to a Japanese bar and had a beer. Then Naomi took Daniel to Shinjuku, a trendy shopping district in Tokyo, where he bought a shirt. It was a small shirt, and Daniel had to choose the largest size.

Naomi and Daniel spent lovely afternoons in the city with Kim, who sometimes followed her. She had great success with the last commercial she did with the producers and was therefore invited to produce an album. On her way out, she sometimes met with fans and would sign autographs for them. Daniel was very impressed that he had such a capable girlfriend. Daniel got down on one knee on his last day and proposed to Naomi, who generously accepted. For Daniel, this was the highlight and the happiest moment of his life. They told their parents the good news when they arrived at the house. While Naomi's mother seemed a little worried, Naomi's father was happy because he liked him. Naomi did not tell Daniel that her producers did not want her to get married so soon. As a budding singer who gained fame and popularity, her producers wanted her to remain status quo. However, nothing stopped her from getting engaged, as it did not hurt her reputation. They spent the last night at Naomi's, having dinner and a small celebration.

Chapter 8

Daniel flew home to Munich the next day. Daniel called Liesel and told her the good news when he arrived home. Liesel seemed happy for her father, as she had heard about Naomi being a singer in Japan, as she was now very popular in the United Kingdom due to the publicity she had generated. Over the next few days, Daniel spent his time selling the sweets he had bought. As the sweets were so popular, he had no trouble finding a buyer. Of course, he also gave Naomi some of his sweets to try before he left Japan. She liked them and said they were something special. Daniel went into his study and switched on the computer. He received a brief email from Mr Schalter saying that he had broken up with Diane and that she wanted to return to Daniel. Daniel wrote an equally quick email to Mr Schalter saying that he would not take Diane back under any circumstances and that she would have to stay with him given the ensuing circumstances. After Daniel sent the email, he heard nothing more from Mr Schalter. Daniel did not want to get involved with Diane again and clarified this to Mr Schalter. It disrupted his afternoon as he did not want to hear any more from Diane.

Naomi had finished producing her album and was due to visit Daniel in about two weeks. Daniel wrote back to Naomi and told her he would take her to see her daughter, who was in Bonn. Naomi was very interested in getting to know Liesel, who she had heard a lot about from Daniel. Liesel also listened to Japanese music occasionally and was a fan of Naomi. As Naomi became increasingly popular, Kim travelled to Munich with Naomi in two weeks as a precautionary measure for her safety. Daniel did not mind at all, as he had taken a liking to the quiet Kim, who drove them everywhere during his stay in Tokyo. Naomi flew to Munich two weeks later to spend some time with Daniel. Kim carried her bags into his house. Daniel showed him to the guest room, where he stowed his luggage.

Meanwhile, Mr Schmidt looked out his window and saw Naomi approaching Daniel's house. He was surprised that he had found someone so quickly, but he did not dare ask him who it was. Daniel made Naomi and Kim something for lunch. They had pasta with Bolognese sauce. They ate together, and Daniel asked how Kim liked Munich. Kim said he had never been here before and wanted to explore the area. Daniel said they were going to Bonn and that he could show Kim many sights there, too. Kim smiled softly at him and nodded. The following day, the group took the train to Bonn Central Station. It was the day that Daniel didn't have to work. He took the time to show Naomi the sights while their relationship was still in its early stages. Naomi looked tired from the long flight, and everyone had an early night.

Chapter 9

Daniel drove Naomi and Kim to the station the following morning, where they took the train to Bonn. When they reached Bonn, Liesel was waiting for them at the station, as Andrea had to work that morning. Both girls were surprised to see each other. Liesel smiled warmly at Naomi and said she was prettier in real life than on television. Naomi gave Liesel her newly produced album. They all arrived at Andrea's house. Liesel told her father she was engaged to Johannes, who had proposed. Daniel was pleased to hear this. He was happier than ever before. Liesel did not tell her father that she was now pregnant. She did not want to let the secret out of the bag, but Naomi noticed something lit up in her face.

Meanwhile, Liesel and Johannes were looking for an apartment in Bonn. With their wedding coming up in autumn, they found a house near the train station, a four-bedroom apartment with big windows and a massive door. It cost about eight hundred thousand dollars. Johannes had help from his father, who could afford the apartment. While Johannes worked, Liesel was expected to stay home for at least the first two years of the baby's life. When Liesel finally told her father she was pregnant, Daniel was amazed and a little worried, as he had not expected to become a grandfather so soon. Meanwhile, Kim, who had witnessed the whole scenario, congratulated Liesel. Liesel also showed Daniel and Naomi her new apartment near the station. Daniel asked who had bought the apartment, and Liesel said it was Johannes's father who had bought it. Daniel was taken aback when he finally realised that his little daughter was all grown up and would soon be a mother. The group spent two pleasant days in Bonn. Andrea drove them to the hotel where Liesel worked, where they had dinner. After dinner, Liesel brought out a cake that she had personally decorated. It was a giant chocolate cake with pink icing in the shape of roses on top. Daniel was very impressed. Johannes meanwhile said that the cost of the wedding would be on them. Naomi and Daniel were invited to the wedding, including Kim, who smiled. The wedding was to occur in autumn in October at the hotel where Liesel worked. Daniel also met with Johannes' father at his family's dinner at his house. Daniel and Johannes' father, Richard, got along very well. Daniel was very pleased with the course of events. He had heard nothing more from Mr Schalter after he had sent him the email. Daniel was also supposed to pay part of the wedding costs, but Richard would not hear of it. It was the first wedding in Richards family, as Johannes was also an only child. His mother had died when Johannes was four years old. Johannes had always looked for a mother figure, but he was lucky to meet Liesel, who cared for him when he became ill. Daniel, Naomi, and Kim travelled to Bonn shortly after dinner at Johannes's house. They would see each other again in October for the wedding. In the meantime, Daniel had left some sweets for Liesel and Johannes, which he had supposedly bought in Melbourne. They all tried the sweets and found that they tasted sweet, sour and yet delicious. It became increasingly popular in Germany, where many people bought it as a snack and even to eat during the day. Daniel, as the man who had awoken from the wreckage of his marriage to Diane, meant something for him and Naomi, not only a new beginning for Liesel. It was the wedding of the year, and Naomi had already booked her tickets to Munich to attend the wedding. With Naomi, he felt he had met the right person, as he did not mind that she had a career ahead of her and did not think he should rush to get married again. As his fiancée, Naomi held him in high esteem and was very happy about his marriage proposal.

On October 17, the big day finally arrived. The bride looked radiant in her dress, and Johannes wiped his forehead with a handkerchief as he looked nervous. It was the first wedding in a long time. The guests were invited to the hotel, where they had dinner after a long church service. The happy couple cut a vanilla cake with pink icing flowers at dinner. It was a three-tier cake. Everyone at the wedding reception was served a slice of cake. Daniel thought it was delicious. Naomi, who wore a blue off-the-shoulder dress, thought it was just as beautiful. She sang at the wedding to the applause of the guests while Daniel played the piano. The guests drank champagne and ate plenty of roast chicken for dinner. Many danced during the party, and Daniel and Naomi also danced to the music of *When I Fall in Love*. Daniel had never been so happy. He had semi-retired as he felt he was now a little too old to travel around the world tasting sweets. At the wedding reception, sweets were everywhere on the table for the guests. For Daniel, he would spend some time with Naomi before their big day. As Naomi pursued her career, he understood that the producers wanted her job to be successful. It was a challenging road, as the competition in Japan was fierce. However, as her international career took off, the producers became more confident in Naomi as an international singer. As an international singer, Daniel would partner with her on her travels. Naomi was expected to travel to China and even England to perform concerts. Daniel welcomed his new role as a supportive partner for Naomi, which did not exist in his relationship with Diane. However, this was a relationship Daniel believed in more. Their culture resembled the shared love between the two parties. Although there were many attractions throughout Naomi's career, she remained faithful to Daniel. Daniel was determined to have children with Naomi one day. As a dual citizen of Germany and Japan, Naomi had the right to remain in Germany as a citizen, although she rarely spoke about it. Geopolitical factors would influence her decision on where to stay if she married. Daniel was willing to move to Japan if Naomi's parents objected to her previous move to Germany. He did not want Naomi to sacrifice her time and citizenship and was willing to travel to Japan to stay. Daniel knew it would be easier to move to Japan as he was half Japanese.

The wedding ended at midnight. Many of the guests left then. Liesel and Johannes would spend their honeymoon in Austria and go in the morning. Daniel and Naomi said goodbye to them. They were also due to travel back to Japan the following day, as Daniel had decided to stay in Japan for the time being. As a man who had recovered from the nightmare of his previous marriage, he was glad that he made the right decisions and took the right opportunities that came his way. Daniel and Naomi drove to the airport in Düsseldorf to catch the flight to Japan. It would be a twelve-hour journey straight to Japan. Naomi's parents would pick her up at the airport. Naomi had another concert to give in Osaka before her trip to Tokyo. The happy couple boarded the plane while Daniel closed his eyes and dozed for a while in his familiarity as a traveller. Naomi looked lovingly at Daniel and knew that their impending marriage would last for a long, long time.